Percy the Park Keeper
A·B·C

NICK BUTTERWORTH

Collins

An Imprint of HarperCollinsPublishers

First published in Great Britain by HarperCollins Publishers Ltd in 1998

1 3 5 7 9 10 8 6 4 2

ISBN: 0 00 664667 0

Illustrations copyright © Nick Butterworth 1989, 1992, 1993, 1994, 1995, 1996, 1997, 1998

Text copyright © HarperCollins Publishers 1998

The illustrator asserts the moral right to be identified as the illustrator of the work.

Printed and bound in Singapore by Imago

Hello! I'm Percy the Park Keeper!
Would you like to play I-Spy in my
park? It will help you to learn your
A B C, and you can meet all my
animal friends along the way.
Turn the page to start the game.

A a

I spy something
beginning with a...

They're my friends who live in
the park with me.

animals

B b

I spy something beginning with b...

He's black and white – and sometimes he needs a bath!

badger

C c

I spy something
beginning with c...

I always wear this when it's cold.

coat

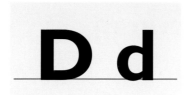

D d

I spy something
beginning with **d**...

They make a noise like this: QUACK!

ducks

E e

I spy something
beginning with e…

This rabbit is my friend.
He is very proud of his long…

ears

F f

I spy something
beginning with **f**...

Lots of these grow in the park in spring.

flowers

G g

I spy something
beginning with g . . .

It's green and we all love lying on it!

grass

H h

I spy something
beginning with **h** . . .

He's the prickliest animal in the park!

hedgehog

 **I i**

I spy something
beginning with i…

Can you see some of these
hanging from my window?

icicles

J j

I spy something beginning with j . . .

I think it's time I bought a new one.

jug

K k

I spy something
beginning with **k**...

I use it to make a cup of tea!

kettle

L l

I spy something
beginning with l...

Look at them blowing by!

leaves

Mm

I spy something beginning with m...

He lives underground - and is very good at digging!

mole

N n

I spy something
beginning with **n**...

A mouse is sitting on the end of
the badger's...

nose

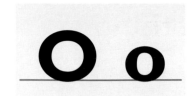 **O o**

I spy something beginning with o...

The mice have used one of these for their snowman's nose!

orange

P p

I spy something
beginning with p...

You might get this through the post!
I wonder what's in it?

parcel

Q q

I spy something
beginning with **q**...

This keeps you nice and warm
in the winter!

quilt

R r

I spy something
beginning with **r**...

This friend of mine
loves jumping.

rabbit

S s

I spy something
beginning with s...

I'm looking after him because
he's hurt his arm.

squirrel

T t

I spy something
beginning with t...

They often come in handy in the park.

tools

U u

I spy something
beginning with **u**...

They are white with pink spots.
Can you see them on the line?

underpants

V v

I spy something
beginning with **v**...

Flowers look very pretty in this!

vase

 Ww

I spy something beginning with w...

I always have something to carry in mine.

wheelbarrow

X x

I spy something
ending with **x** . . .

He's one of my friends and he
lives in the park.

fo**x**

Y y

I spy something beginning with **y** . . .

I like having this for my lunch!

yoghurt

Z z

I spy something
beginning with z...

I wonder how he came into
the park!

zebra

Here's Percy's
alphabet.

A a

E e   **F f**   **G g**

K k   **L l**   **M m**

Q q   **R r**   **S s**

V v   **W w**   **X x**

B b C c D d

H h I i J j

N n O o P p

T t U u

Y y Z z

*Read all about Percy and his animal friends
and see them on TV and video too!*

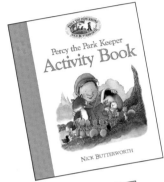

Percy the Park Keeper
Activity Book

NICK BUTTERWORTH

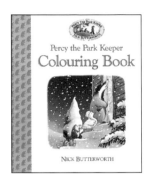

Percy the Park Keeper
Colouring Book

NICK BUTTERWORTH

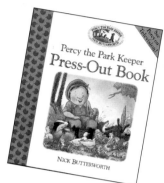

Percy the Park Keeper
Press-Out Book

NICK BUTTERWORTH

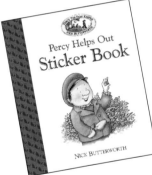

Percy Helps Out
Sticker Book

NICK BUTTERWORTH

Percy the Park Keeper
Story & Sticker Book

NICK BUTTERWORTH

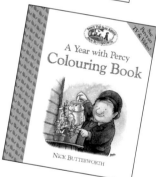

A Year with Percy
Colouring Book

NICK BUTTERWORTH

ONE SNOWY NIGHT

NICK BUTTERWORTH

AFTER THE STORM

NICK BUTTERWORTH
WITH FOLD-OUT POSTER

THE RESCUE PARTY

NICK BUTTERWORTH

THE SECRET PATH

NICK BUTTERWORTH
WITH FOLD-OUT POSTER

THE TREASURE HUNT

NICK BUTTERWORTH